This
Treasure Cove Story
belongs to

THE MIGHTY THOR

A CENTUM BOOK 978-1-912841-41-7
Published in Great Britain by Centum Books Ltd.
This edition published 2019.

3 5 7 9 10 8 6 4 2

Centum Books Ltd, 20 Devon Square, Newton Abbot, Devon, TQ12 2HR, UK.
9/10 Fenian St, Dublin 2, D02 RX24, Ireland.

www.centumbooksltd.co.uk | books@centumbooksltd.co.uk
CENTUM BOOKS Limited Reg. No. 07641486.

A CIP catalogue record for this book is available
from the British Library.

Printed in China.

A Treasure Cove Story

MARVEL

THE MIGHTY THOR

Adapted by Billy Wrecks
Based on the Marvel comic book series THOR
Illustrated by the Storybook Art Group

Far away, in the land of *Asgard*, brave warriors fought ogres, trolls, dragons, frost giants and monsters of all kinds.

The bravest, **strongest** warrior in all of *Asgard* was named Thor. No monster could withstand his **might**!

Thor's father, Odin, was the king of Asgard!
Odin was **proud** of his brave son.

Odin showed Thor the most **powerful** weapon in the land…

a magical hammer called **Mjolnir**
(pronounced *mee-ALL-neer*).

Thor tried to lift the hammer.
But even with his great
strength, he could not!

Odin told Thor that only a truly **valiant** warrior could lift the hammer.

Thor vowed to become
a hero worthy of the
mighty hammer.

Thor fought many **powerful** foes...

... and he was **VICTORIOUS** in every battle.

He even fought a *dragon*.

After many adventures, Thor felt he was a worthy **warrior**.

Thor went to Odin's palace and told his father that he was ready to try to lift **Mjolnir** once again.

As the people of Asgard watched, Thor lifted the **heavy** hammer into the air. He *was* worthy!

With the magical hammer, Thor could control **thunder**, *lightning* and **wind**.

By spinning the
hammer over his head,
Thor could even **soar**
through the air!

The **mighty** Thor vowed that he would always use his **strength** and his **powerful** hammer to fight for good.